MW00881212

GLOBETROTTER

Meridien

Travels the world

Claire Wilby

Globetrotter Publishing Limited

www.meridientravelstheworld.co.uk

First published in 2021 by Globetrotter Publishing
Limited
Text by Claire Wilby, text copyright @ Globetrotter
Publishing Limited 2021

Illustrations by Antony Wootten, illustrations
copyright @ Globetrotter Publishing Limited 2021

ISBN 978-1-9168787-0-9

To Esme,
Enjoy Meridien's Journey!

Claire
x

For
Alexandra and Dennis
(Meridien's Grandparents)

Contents

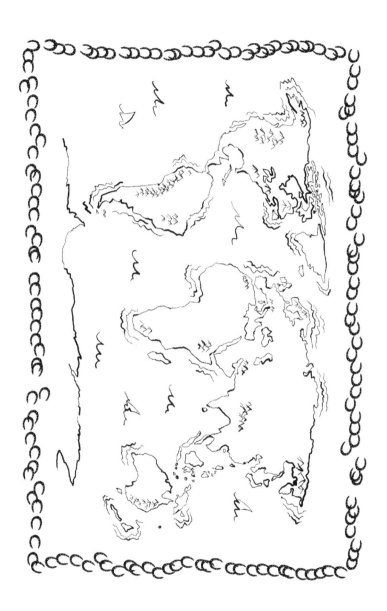

First Wobbly Steps

France

Bonjour!
(French for 'Hello!')

The journey begins in France one fine spring morning.

It was the second of April, the day after April Fools' Day. In a grassy paddock in a town called St

Martin in the Loire Valley, a beautiful mare gave birth to a stunning long-legged colt, a boy horse: a chestnut foal with a golden shimmer.

Mother nature gives horses incredible instinct and within a few minutes, the future globetrotter, Monsieur Meridien de St Martin, took his first wobbly steps of what was going to be an epic journey.

Known by his friends as Meridien, he has a big white blaze and three white socks. From a leggy foal, he grew to stand over 17 hands high. He is a very tall chap.

His early years in France were like those of Black Beauty in England many years before: happy, easy days. He would play with other young horses and gallop freely in the green pastures. Then the time came for him to leave behind his carefree life and become a show jumper. A show jumper headed for the bright lights of the international arena.

Meridien's first journey was an exotic one. At the age of six he was sent, with his passport, to Paris, in a big horsebox. The journey did not stop there. In Paris he got on his first aeroplane, the first of many. Leaving the temperate climes of Europe behind him, he landed in the hot and steamy desert of Qatar.

First Steps in the Sand - and Charlie

Qatar

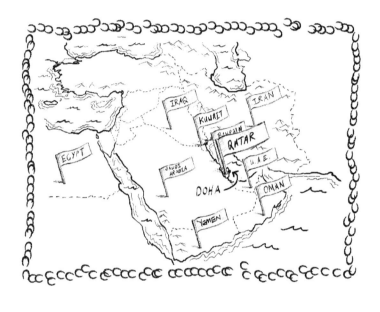

As-salamu alaykum!
(Arabic for 'Peace be upon you!')

Meridien had been used to lush green pastures. It must have been quite a surprise when he arrived in the sandy desert. On arrival in Doha, the capital city of Qatar, the only green to be seen was the green of the leaves of the palm trees dotted around the country. Little did he know how important those palm trees would become later in his life.

His new home was like a palace. Not like Versailles, the big palace the horsebox had driven past in France on Meridien's journey to the airport in Paris, but an Arabian palace, with domes, turrets and towers - all shiny and new.

He arrived in Qatar at the height of summer and Doha was very, very, very hot - it was so hot you could fry an egg on the pavement! It was much hotter than even the hottest summer's day in his old home in France. He had air-conditioning in his stable - quite the luxury! Even the big arena the horses were ridden in had big fans to cool down the hot desert air.

Meridien had travelled on the plane from Paris with two other horses - big bay racehorses called Whisper and Warrior. They did not come to the same new home in Doha. Whisper and Warrior were headed to a racing stables owned by the King of Qatar, 'the Emir'.

Meridien was a long way from home and all alone for the first time. However, although he was all alone and a long way from the only home he had ever known, he quickly made lots of new friends in his new stables.

This was a whole new world and life was very different from what he had been used to. There was no playing and galloping in green pastures. Early in the mornings he would be taken out of his stable for exercise before the sun came up - any later and it was far too hot for him as he had been used to a much colder climate. There was lots of jumping practice to get him fit and ready for competitions. Then munching hay and resting in his air-conditioned stable, surrounded by all his new friends.

Most weekends he would fly on planes to other countries and cities with some of his new friends to take part in competitions. He soon collected stamps in his passport from Saudi Arabia, Bahrain and the United Arab Emirates and he competed in the capital cities of all of these countries. Meridien, the globetrotter, was busy trotting the globe, collecting rosettes and trophies.

One day Meridien was show jumping at a competition in Abu Dhabi in the United Arab Emirates. There he was spotted by a young English girl, Charlotte - Charlie to her friends - who was looking to find a riding and travel partner - a horse to trot around the globe with. She knew the moment she saw his big white blaze and his smiling eyes that he was the right horse for her.

Charlie went up to Meridien who reached out and nuzzled her shoulder affectionately. She introduced herself to Meridien's rider, who she could see had come from Doha as he had a Qatari flag on his riding helmet.

She asked, a little cheekily, 'Is this beautiful horse for sale? I'd love for him to stay with me here in Abu Dhabi!'

Meridien's rider, slightly taken by surprise at Charlie's boldness, replied, 'Actually, you are in luck!'

Charlie gasped excitedly, 'Really?'

The Qatari rider continued, 'Meridien - that's his name - has been show jumping internationally for several years now and deserves a change. We'd like him to have more variety in his life. So, yes, he is looking for a new home!'

Charlie could not have been happier, 'I promise Meridien will have lots and lots of variety and a very happy home with me,' she said as she reached her arms around Meridien's neck to give him a big hug.

 Charlie began to cry tears of joy, emotional at the thought of this new friendship and the journey they were about to begin. Exciting travels that nobody could have imagined when Meridien first stumbled clumsily to his feet early on that April morning back in France.

That evening, Charlie took Meridien to his new home at the Old Palace Stables in Abu Dhabi where a kind Argentinian vet made sure he was in good health. He passed all the tests and checks with flying colours.

Meridien also revealed his gentle character and his especially calm temperament when the kind Argentinian vet's littlest daughter, Lola, who was with her father that evening, asked, 'Please can I sit on the big horsey?'

Charlie smiled and nodded, 'If your Dad says it's ok, it's fine by me!'

The kind Argentinian vet lifted Lola up onto Meridien's back. Despite Lola's excited whooping and wriggling, Meridien was as cool as a cucumber and did not bat an eyelid!

*

Since that first evening, as you are about to find out, Meridien and Charlie have been on quite a journey...

Ahlan! - and Ali

United Arab Emirates

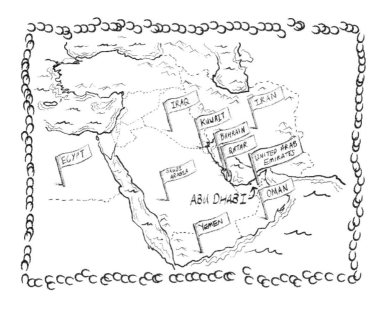

Ahlan!
(Arabic for 'Welcome!')

Ahlan! Welcome! - as it says on big signs when you arrive in Abu Dhabi, the capital city of the United Arab Emirates. Meridien really was welcomed in Abu Dhabi. Welcomed with open arms to a new home in the next chapter of his journey.

Meridien's sandy coloured stable was in a line of twelve in a beautiful quiet part of the Old Palace Stables. He had new friends to the left and new friends to the right. It was hot like in Doha, but he arrived in April - the day after his birthday - so it was still cool enough for him to have a stable with just a fan whirring away overhead. The stable was open, both front and back, to allow the breeze to flow through and help keep him cool. It looked out onto a row of date palms, like the palm trees he had first seen in Doha. Sand paddocks lay beyond them to the front, and a whole series of sand arenas to the back.

On his first morning at the Old Palace Stables, Meridien was introduced to his new groom, Ali, who would care for Meridien when Charlie was not able to be there. He was to become one of Meridien's best and most trusted friends. He treated Meridien like royalty - he was now living at the Old Palace Stables after all! Ali would take him on walks around the sandy date palm garden, hose him off with chilled water to cool him down from the desert heat, groom him and talk to him as he kept him company in his stable. Ali spoke some English but was from Pakistan and spoke another language that Meridien had never heard before, Urdu. But Ali and Meridien communicated in their own special language. There were never any misunderstandings.

That first morning at his new home at the Old Palace Stables in Abu Dhabi, it was hard to know if it was the sound of the call to prayer from the nearby mosque or the loud grumbling of his tummy in anticipation of breakfast that woke Meridien (Meridien was always hungry!). The sound of the chanting of the call to prayer carried across from the Old Palace Stables' mosque only a few hundred metres from Meridien's stable. Five times a day, at each call to prayer, Ali and the other grooms walked across to the mosque for their moment of reflection and prayer. For Meridien, when he heard the first call to prayer of the day, he would know it was nearly time for breakfast. The second meant that it was time for lunch. The third would usually wake him from his afternoon nap and the fourth meant dinner time. By the time the gentle chanting of the fifth and final call reached his stable, he was usually in a deep, dreamy sleep. When he heard the first, the second and the fourth calls, he would start whinnying as a gentle reminder to his friend Ali that when he had said his prayers and returned from the mosque - it was feeding time!

On returning from the mosque that first morning, Ali turned Meridien out into the sand paddock in front of his stable for the first time. Catching new, unknown scents in the air, Meridien fluttered his nostrils in excitement and took off around the paddock at a gallop. A very, very fast gallop. Then slid through the sand as he put the brakes on and came to a halt just before the paddock fence. He left only millimetres to spare. He wanted to explore, to take in all the new sights and sounds. Again, he galloped and galloped, round and round the paddock. He threw in a buck and a squeal and then called to the other horses, his new friends. They all thought this was great fun and joined in.

Suddenly, Meridien stopped his antics - he had spotted the big heap of hay in the corner of the paddock. Once he had seen that it was head down and munch. Nothing could distract him now. He was quiet until it was time for Ali to take him back to his stable before the heat of the desert sun reached the paddock.

Sweet Treats

United Arab Emirates

Meridien was settling in well and was very much at home at the Old Palace Stables. When Charlie approached his stable in the mornings, his ears would prick up and he would give off a low soft whinny, his nostrils fluttering - his morning '*Ahlan*', 'Welcome', to Charlie. Charlie's '*Ahlan*' to Meridien was one of the mints she always had tucked away in her pocket for him. He learnt quickly  where the mints were kept and would snuffle around in search of them at every chance he got.

One morning when the date palms in front of Meridien's stable were ready to harvest, a date dropped from one of the tall trees. It landed in front of Charlie on the ground. She bent down and picked it up.

'Look Meridien, it's a date! Fresh from the tree!' she said walking towards him, holding the date in her hand.

Not for long! Meridien extended his long neck over the stable door and hoovered up the date from the palm of her hand, stone and all, nodding his head up and down with approval.

Charlie laughed. 'You want more, don't you!' she said to her new four-legged friend.

She walked back towards the date palms to look for another fallen date, but there were none. A whinny of encouragement came from behind her. So, of course, she climbed one of the trees to collect more dates for him. The Arabian horses at the  stables also liked the dates but having grown up in the desert they were used to them. They had learnt to spit out the stones, just as humans spit out cherry stones. Although Meridien saw how his friends pitted the dates and spat out the stones, in the same way that you cannot teach an old dog new tricks (not that Meridien was old), this was just not something that he was able to learn to do.

There was no turning back from this moment. Meridien had found his favourite treat. From that day onwards, if Meridien saw Charlie near the date palms, he would whinny softly in the hope of getting his date - which of course he always did! Charlie became chief tree climber, date collector and date-pitter: full-service date delivery for Meridien.

Mints and dates. Meridien's new life was full of wonderful, sweet treats. It was in Abu Dhabi that Meridien's own travelling sweet shop came to be. At the local souk, the market in the centre of the city, Charlie had found a small wooden trunk with a globe engraved on the top - perfect for a globetrotter. She bought it to store Meridien's treats in and to take with them when they went on their globe trots. Having a travelling sweet shop meant that the memories of the places they visited could be kept alive in the form of treats. First it was filled with mints and dates but there was plenty of space for more.

An Unwelcome Guest

United Arab Emirates

Abu Dhabi is mainly desert, and, unlike back in France, there were not many fields of grass from which to make hay. It was not possible to make enough hay locally to feed all the horses, so scrumptious hay was flown in from the green fields of Kentucky in the United States of America by plane to the United Arab Emirates - hay flown across the ocean to feed the horses in the desert.

One day in August, Meridien's hay was not quite up to its usual standard. It was not the hay from Kentucky, it was the local hay. It was not juicy. It was dry. But he was hungry, so he kept munching.

Suddenly he leapt back in his stable, crashing against the back wall. What was on his nose? Was it still on his nose? Was it all over his head? Was it crawling up between his eyes? What was it?

Meridien jumped around his stable, bucking and squealing. He made quite a racket with his thrashing around. Ali ran over to find Meridien with his head fully submerged in his water bucket, splashing water all over the place.

'Calm down boy!' Ali said as he dashed into his stable.

But Meridien did not want to calm down. From his nostrils to the top of his neck, Meridien's head was swelling up. He was starting to look more like an elephant than a horse!

'You poor boy! You are so hot and sweaty. And your face....your face is swelling up like a balloon!' Ali said with a worried look. 'Were you trying to cool it down with the water from the bucket? Let me get help.'

Charlie arrived at the stables, planning to take Meridien out for a ride. She was startled as she saw his swollen face.

'What's going on? What has happened to Meridien?' she called out, overcome with worry.

She started to panic.

'It's OK! I've already called the kind Argentinian vet. He's on his way,' Ali told Charlie, trying to comfort her.

As soon as the vet arrived, he dashed to Meridien's stable and inspected his swollen head.

'He has been stung on the nose by a scorpion,' he told Ali and Charlie.

A scorpion! It had been hiding in the less than tasty hay.

The kind Argentinian vet gave Meridien some delicious medicine that tasted of dates, only sweeter. Meridien nodded his head up and down in appreciation and seemed much better as soon as he swallowed it. It worked like magic.

It was a few days before the swelling went down. The kind Argentinian vet came regularly to give Meridien the delicious medicine. Very quickly his usual appetite returned and soon he was munching hay again.

After the unfortunate incident with the scorpion, only sumptuous Kentucky hay was served for Meridien to munch on!

Desert Crossing

Amongst the Dunes

Early one morning, after breakfast, a HUGE green suitcase appeared in front of Meridien's stable. Charlie was packing it with his saddles and bridles and putting lots of bags of sweet dates from the date palms in front of his stable into his travelling sweet shop. A very big, very long white horsebox arrived.

Meridien whinnied farewell to his friends as he bounded up the ramp of the horsebox, excited at the prospect of another journey. The other horses kept whinnying as the horsebox drove away and Meridien called back to them. As a globetrotter, there was a very good chance Meridien would meet his friends again somewhere on his world travels, so this was not goodbye, just farewell for now.

As he had grown so fond of him, Ali did not want to have to say goodbye to Meridien. He asked to continue looking after Meridien and join him and Charlie on their journey across the desert to their new destination. Charlie was delighted that Meridien's trusted friend would still be there for him in their new home.

For hours they drove through an empty desert, with only camels and goats to break up the lines in the sand. The colour of the sand varied from bright yellow to deep red and grew from plains into big dunes. It was beautiful.

It was a very long and hot journey - about six or seven hours with stops along the way for water. The first time Charlie went to take Meridien off the horsebox, to give him a chance to stretch his legs and have some water, he froze at the top of the ramp. He

did not want to budge. His nostrils were twitching. He was not happy. Then Charlie saw what Meridien had seen: a caravan of camels drifting through the desert, only a few metres across the road from where they had parked. There were about twenty fully grown camels moving steadily through the sand and six or so baby camels weaving in and out between them.

Although Meridien had been living in the desert for many years now, he had never come this close to camels. They must have given off a scent that told Meridien to be wary, and wary he was.

Eventually, Ali and Charlie coaxed Meridien down the ramp with some dates, but he was keen to get back into the horsebox and drive away from the camels as quickly as possible.

Fortunately, as the journey progressed, Meridien learnt that he did not have to be scared of coming down the ramp and he started to enjoy the little breaks and all the new sights.

At the end of their long journey through the desert, the horsebox came to a stop at their destination and the ramp opened. Meridien had arrived in the beautiful city of Muscat in the Sultanate of Oman.

Meridien the Racehorse?

Oman

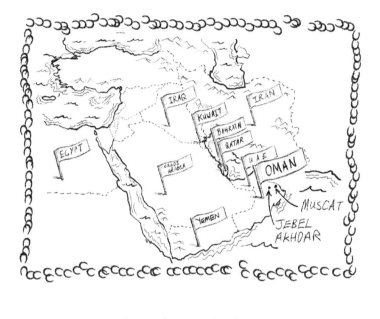

As-salamu alaykum!
(Arabic for 'Peace be upon you!')

Meridien quickly settled into his new home in Muscat, the capital city of the Sultanate of Oman. It was just as hot as in Abu Dhabi but felt different. From his new stables, just outside the city, he could see mountains - craggy, rocky mountains, that turned pink at sunrise and at sunset. The stables were close to the palace of the Sultan, the King and Ruler of the Sultanate of Oman, where he lived with his wife, the beautiful Sultana.

Across the road from the stables was a racetrack.

'Would you take us across to the racetrack one morning?' Charlie asked her new Omani friend Lina - known as little Lina, as she was so tiny, especially compared to her very tall ex-racehorse Hank from Texas.

'We can let Meridien *try his hoof* at racing,' Charlie added, laughing.

'Absolutely! Hank would love that. He can show Meridien the ropes,' little Lina said. 'Let's sneak across early tomorrow morning when no one is around. We will have the racetrack all to ourselves!'

The next day, the girls set off on their racing adventure at sunrise as planned. Meridien was very brave and did not shy or jump around as Charlie rode him over the big, wide, tarmac road to get across to the racetrack.

His new friend Hank was not nearly as calm. He danced and pranced around on the road, jumping from side to side and snorting.

'Hank can see monsters!' little Lina told Charlie, giggling, as she bounced around in the saddle. Charlie, happy to be riding Meridien who was walking calmly alongside his skittish friend, laughed too.

'I think he knows we are on our way to the racetrack and it's bringing back memories of his days competing as a racehorse,' little Lina told Charlie.

As soon as they were away from the road and onto the grass, little Lina shouted, in Arabic, '*Yallah*!', which means, 'let's go!'

And they were off. They started head-to-head, neck and neck, together. Charlie pushed Meridien on to keep up with Hank who was quickly lengths ahead, but Meridien soon remembered that he was not a racehorse like Hank. He was a show jumper. He was built for leaping over fences not racing along gallops. It was fun but he just wanted to enjoy the journey, so he slowed down to a sedate canter.

Suddenly, the sprinklers around the racetrack turned on and water sprayed all over Meridien. He bolted. Taken by surprise at Meridien's sudden speed, Charlie clung on tightly and just about managed not to fall off. However, once Meridien felt the cooling effect of the water spraying all over him, he slowed down. Hot and sweaty from the desert sun, the spray was rather refreshing, so he stopped

to stand by the sprinkler to enjoy a welcome shower - and Charlie was soaked from head to toe.

Little Lina, noticing that Meridien and Charlie were no longer galloping along with her and Hank, came back to a walk. She turned to look over her shoulder and saw Meridien and Charlie way back down the racetrack, standing in the spray of the sprinkler. She couldn't help but laugh.

Trotting back towards them, she called out, 'I guess Meridien doesn't want to be a racehorse!'

Charlie smiled. 'I think you are right little Lina. We will stick to show jumping for now!'

Pomegranates and Prizes

Oman

Just before Meridien was to embark on the next leg of his journey, leaving the desert and the Middle East behind him, Ruth, Charlie's absolutely fabulous show jumping trainer, signed them up for a very special competition.

Their journey to the competition, after sunset, once the heat of the day had subsided, took them through the desert. The further they travelled away from the city of Muscat and the deeper they went into the desert, the more sand there was in the air. The sand irritated Meridien's eyes, but Charlie had learnt that she could soothe his eyes with cold tea bags to take away the sting, which she would always do after a journey in the desert. He really was pampered!

After just a couple of hours, they arrived on the top of a beautiful green mountain - yes, a green mountain in the desert, an oasis. It was even called 'Green Mountain' - or '*Jebel Akhdar*' in Arabic. It was like nowhere Meridien or Charlie had ever been before. There were apricot trees, beautiful roses of all different colours and rows and rows of

32

pomegranate trees, abundant with fruit. There were also goats, lots of goats. The goats bleated loudly and mingled amongst the people and the horses, fearless and hopeful of snatching someone's sandwich.

There were beautiful stables for the hundreds of horses who had come for the competition. An arena the size of a football pitch was lit up by floodlights and the moonlight, and a traditional music group were playing drums, zithers and lyres. Small children were dancing enthusiastically to the beat of the drums, the zinging of the zither and the strumming of the lyre.

Ali stayed by the horses whilst Charlie went with Ruth and the other riders and trainers to walk the course of show jumps. As riders, they needed to learn the course of jumps off by heart. Charlie and Ruth chatted about how fast Charlie should let Meridien go, how best to cut corners and how many strides to take between each fence.

'Just remember everything we have practised at home and you will be in the ribbons,' Ruth encouraged Charlie, 'Meridien will love these jumps!'

Back at the stables, Ali was grooming Meridien and getting him smartened-up.

'Today is a very special day, my friend,' Ali said to Meridien.

He knew that Meridien would soon be flying away to pastures new.

'I'm not going to be able to come with you when you leave Muscat, as I can't go too far away from my family who need me here in the Middle East,' Ali told Meridien. 'Let's make you look especially smart for this special day and make it a day to remember,' Ali said.

He proceeded to cut Meridien's mane so that it was as straight as an arrow. It looked as though he had used a ruler to cut it as straight as possible. He also cut his forelock, using the same precision, and Meridien's new look fringe appeared!

'Charlie, look!' Ali grinned as Charlie returned from walking the course with Ruth, pointing to Meridien.

The new look took Charlie a little by surprise. It really did look a little odd, but Ali was so proud of Meridien's new trim. Charlie could not be cross. She smiled.

'Thank you, Ali, you have made him all smart,' she said as she went to put on Meridien's saddle and bridle, ready for the competition.

Meridien had travelled to the Green Mountain with his very tall ex-racehorse friend Hank from Texas. Hank was always more excitable than Meridien, who was older and, if not always wiser, was definitely calmer. As the two horses headed to the warm-up arena, Hank's eyes were on stalks! Meridien, giving off his calming influence, tried to convince Hank that there were no monsters out there to be scared of. Hank pranced and danced, bouncing little Lina around in the saddle whilst Ruth helped Meridien and Charlie with their final warm-up over the practice jumps.

'You go girl! You've got this!' Charlie heard Ruth saying as she cantered Meridien past her into the football pitch sized arena.

Feeling confident, Meridien and Charlie took in the vibrant atmosphere as they cantered around. Ruth joined Charlie's friends from the Old Palace Stables in Abu Dhabi who had come to Oman to watch and who were picnicking under the apricot trees to the side of the arena.

All around the arena were pictures of the Sultan and the Sultana who had organised the splendid competition at the amazing location on the Green Mountain. A shiny white 4x4 vehicle parked in the middle of the arena glistened under a bright spotlight - the prize for the winner of the whole competition. Charlie had never seen anything quite like it and had certainly never been to such a grand competition!

As soon as Meridien heard the bell ring, announcing that they could start jumping, he gave off a little squeal of joy. This was his moment. He grew wings - like Pegasus, the famous winged horse from Greek mythology - and was ready to fly. He waited for a sign from Charlie, a gentle squeeze of her calves on his sides, and then they were off.The jumps were extravagant and brightly coloured: some were built to look like red brick walls, others like Arabic style coffee cups, others still resembled a desert scene with date palms to each side - fortunately, this was one time when Meridien was so focused that he did not stop to think about eating dates!

Meridien and Charlie flew around the course, all clear - not a pole touched. A sign from Charlie to slow down and Meridien knew his job was done. As always, after a round of jumps, Meridien could not resist another squeal, accompanied by a buck.

Fortunately, for Charlie in the saddle, just a small one.

There were cheers from the spectators and Ruth came running across to congratulate Charlie and give Meridien a well-deserved date.

Then came the prize-giving. Meridien had won the shiny white 4x4 vehicle, but more importantly for him, his prize also included a big box of dates, apricots and pomegranates. It turned out that Meridien's short mane and new fringe had brought him luck - his lucky haircut!

Charlie was so happy and proud of Meridien, her very special globetrotter friend.

Amazing as it was, Charlie had no use for a shiny white 4x4 vehicle. Once she had taken Meridien back to the stables to be washed off and brushed, she asked Ali to take a seat on a hay bale next to Meridien's stable.

'Close your eyes and hold out your hands,' she told Ali.

He was unsure but saw Meridien nodding his head up and down behind Charlie, so he did as he was told. Charlie placed the keys to the shiny white 4x4 in Ali's hands and took a step back.

'You can open your eyes now,' she said.

Opening his eyes Ali saw the keys.

'Really? For me?' he asked Charlie.

'Meridien would not have it any other way,' said Charlie, and Meridien gave off a soft whinny.

That evening, Ali did not join them in the horsebox as usual, but proudly led the way in his shiny new 4x4.

As they headed home, back to Muscat, delighted with the win for Meridien and a close second place for Hank, Meridien's travelling sweet shop was well stocked with mints, dates and now apricots and pomegranates too. Meridien had not tried the pomegranates, but Charlie was certain he would like them and was saving them to give to him later - although she had packed one to share with Ruth and little Lina on the journey home!

The next day Ali came running up to Charlie, waving a newspaper in the air above his head.

He had quite a spring in his step. He was so excited and spoke so fast that Charlie could not understand a word he was saying. He handed her the newspaper and Charlie shrieked with joy! It was that morning's edition of the Oasis Times and on the front page was a photo of Meridien and Hank at the prize-giving in *Jebel Akhdar*.

The article was written in Arabic.

'Little Lina, I need your help! Look! Come look at this!' Charlie called out to little Lina who was walking towards Meridien's stable with Hank.

'What is it Charlie?' replied little Lina.

'We are famous! We are on the front page of the Oasis Times! What does it say?' Charlie asked little Lina as she showed her the paper.

'Let me see,' said little Lina looking at the article.

She translated for Charlie and Ali: 'Yesterday, an extravagant show jumping event took place in the beautiful oasis on the Green Mountain. Horses came from all over the world to compete and enjoy Omani hospitality. First prize went to the talented Monsieur Meridien de St Martin from France and his English rider Charlie. Second prize went to the Texan horse Hank and his Omani rider little Lina. Congratulations to both - and to all the other horses on their fantastic performances.'

'Amazing, thank you, little Lina! Meridien and Hank are famous!' said Charlie, elated.

Both horses sensed the excitement and started to whinny and nod their heads up and down as Charlie, little Lina and Ali all did a celebration dance in front of the stables.

Plan A and the Mountain Lions

Oman

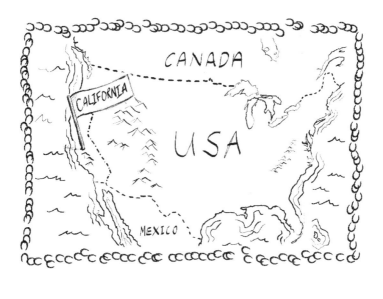

Planning for their next destination in California, Charlie had picked out a beautiful stable for Meridien in the hills above the town of Palo Alto. Views from the arena there looked down onto the San Francisco Bay. A sheriff was on guard at the stables every night. Not because the horses might be stolen but to protect the horses from the mountain lions!

Still in Muscat, waiting to begin the next journey, Meridien made two new friends - Yin and Yang. They were beautiful stallions who had recently arrived in Muscat from America. Yin was black as the night and Yang was white as snow. They were a perfect pair. They had come to perform at a royal party in Muscat and were scheduled to fly back to America a few weeks later. That was ideal, as unlike on Noah's Ark where the animals went in two by two, horses went on a plane in threes, so there was room for Meridien to join Yin and Yang on the flight to his new destination.

However, Yin and Yang's performance at the royal party was so spectacular that they quickly gained lots of fans in Muscat. Two of their biggest fans were Mo and Meriem - little Lina's older twin brother and sister - who just loved Yin and Yang and their tricks. Mo and Meriem had always dreamed of becoming trick riders. Little Lina's parents had bought Hank for her a few years earlier as she wanted to become a jockey. Mo and Meriem pleaded with their parents to keep Yin and Yang and, wanting to support all their children to follow their dreams, they agreed and arranged for the horses to stay with them in Oman.

As Yin and Yang were no longer going back to America but staying with Mo and Meriem, Meridien had to find new travel buddies and a new flight.

Whilst Meridien was waiting to find a new pair of suitable travel companions to take to the skies with, the kind Argentinian vet came all the way from Abu Dhabi to visit. He looked worried.

'I'm so sorry, Charlie. I have some bad news and I wanted to come and explain in person,' said the kind Argentinian vet.

'What is it? What's wrong?' asked Charlie.

'There has been an outbreak of a nasty horse disease in America: *Streptococcus Equi*, also called strangles. As it is very contagious, no horses are allowed to fly there until all the sick horses have been treated,' the kind Argentinian vet explained.

'So we can't fly to California or America at all?' Charlie asked him, quite taken by surprise.

'You will have to put your plans on hold for now Charlie,' the kind Argentinian vet told her, patting Meridien who had popped his head over the stable door to see what was going on.

'Gosh! But that's OK, California may just be a dream for now, but I have a Plan B,' Charlie replied. 'Thank you for coming all this way to warn us.'

'It is always good to have a Plan B, Meridien,' Charlie told her globetrotter, as he nuzzled her pockets looking for treats. 'We will still get to go on another journey, I promise, and as Plan B doesn't involve mountain lions, it is probably a better plan!'

Plan B and the Flying Stable

The Skies

There was quite a kerfuffle around Meridien's stable. All his favourite people were gathered round, fussing over him. There was change in the air. His HUGE green suitcase was packed up outside his stable. Another journey? Where to now?

All his favourite people were sad. They were saying goodbye. There were tears. Ali was being brave and holding back his tears, but he was very quiet. Meridien stretched out his long neck over the stable door and gently nuzzled his friend's shoulder. Ali's eyes welled up and his tears started to flow. Trying to hide his tears from Charlie, Ali led Meridien from the stable towards the horsebox. He wanted these last few minutes by his friend Meridien's side.

Meridien whinnied to all his friends as Ali walked him up the ramp of the horsebox. They whinnied back. Hank, his very tall ex-racehorse friend from Texas, whinnied especially loudly. Meridien was headed off alone, leaving Hank behind, but as a globetrotter, Meridien would surely meet Hank again one day.

'Bye-bye, Little Lina. Please be careful riding Hank,' Charlie said to her Omani friend.

'He'll make a jockey out of me yet!' laughed little Lina.

Charlie turned to Ruth, her absolutely fabulous trainer.

'Thank you for all your help with our show jumping. We could never have won the competition on the Green Mountain without you.'

'Just promise me you will keep up the good work,' Ruth said to Charlie.

Charlie nodded, smiling.

She went to hug them both goodbye, then climbed up into the front of the horsebox.

'See you again somewhere in the world, somewhere on our globe trot,' Charlie said, waving farewell as the horsebox pulled away.

*

Meridien and Charlie were off again. Off to see more of the world.

On the way to the airport the horsebox stopped, and two big bay horses joined Meridien - two racehorses. Meridien whinnied loudly to them - it was Whisper and Warrior, the horses he had flown from Paris to Doha with many years before.

Once they arrived at the airport, Meridien, Whisper and Warrior pranced excitedly off the horsebox and were loaded onto a three-horse trailer: a special trailer for the plane - their flying stable, where they would share the journey until the next destination.

Meridien, Whisper and Warrior were loaded into the flying stable with Meridien's rugs, saddles, the HUGE green suitcase, his travelling sweet shop, hay nets, spare hay nets and, oh, two people were also packed into the flying stable: Charlie and the flying groom (not that the groom actually flies, he is like a flight attendant for horses, to look after them on the flight). Fortunately, Meridien's travel buddies did not have any luggage as Meridien was not travelling light on this journey and there was no more space for anything else in the flying stable.

The flying stable was towed away from the horsebox by a small pick-up truck into a vast hangar. In the hangar was a weighing station with a big set of scales built into the ground. The pilot, who needed to make sure that all the cargo was correctly balanced in the plane, gave a nod of approval. Despite all the luggage and the HUGE green suitcase, they were not overweight!

A very big cargo plane was standing on the runway. The name of the plane was written in big black letters at the front, near the cockpit: **The Ark**.

The flying stable was put onto a scissor lift and - *zig, zag, zig, zag* - was lifted up into The Ark. Meridien munched on his hay whilst Whisper and Warrior jumped around as they were all jerked into the hold, the belly of the cargo plane. Pushed across into the middle of the plane - *clunk, clunk, clunk* -

everything was bolted into place. All other cargo had been loaded - they were ready to fly, ready for the next destination.

Meridien, Whisper and Warrior stood for the whole flight in their flying stable - about seven hours! Charlie was not allowed to stay with Meridien for take-off and landing. She was upstairs in the plush cabin just behind the cockpit made available for rare human passengers on The Ark.

'You can go and visit the horses now. I know that's what you have been waiting for!' the pilot said to Charlie as soon as they were airborne.

'Thank you, thank you, thank you!' Charlie replied enthusiastically as she dashed down the narrow ladder to the hold to check on her precious cargo.

Meridien was just fine. He munched his hay for the entire journey. Whisper and Warrior did not touch theirs, which worked out well for Meridien who cheekily helped himself to their hay too.

The pilot and the co-pilot were not used to having human guests on their cargo plane and they invited Charlie to join them in the cockpit. Charlie entertained them with tales from Meridien's travels and the pilot let her pop up and down to the hold to check on Meridien.

'OK, we are about to land. You can stay with us in the cockpit, but seatbelt on please,' the pilot told Charlie, who fastened her seatbelt excitedly.

She peered out of the cockpit windscreen. They were getting close to their new destination. Charlie had a fantastic view from beside the pilots as the plane started its descent over London. The dawn was just breaking, and a soft light shone across the beautiful bridges dotted along the River Thames. The river was glistening, and the spokes of the London Eye were shining in the morning light.

The Ark landed smoothly and taxied across the runway until they came to a standstill. Charlie rushed down to the hold to check on Meridien. He was unphased by the landing and was still munching his hay. Whisper and Warrior were rather more skittish.

A cold gust of wind blew in as the doors of the hold were opened. It was raining. It was freezing! Meridien had landed in England for the first time. He was back in Europe after many years in the desert.

Back onto a scissor lift - *zig, zag, zig, zag* - Meridien, Whisper and Warrior were lowered from the hold of the plane to the ground where they were loaded onto a horsebox. Charlie and the flying groom headed off through human passport control in the airport and then on to meet the horses for their passport checks.

Meridien and his two racehorse friends were greeted by an official vet at the Heathrow arrivals stables. All the dogs in the quarantine kennels next to the stables seemed to be howling that morning when they arrived, probably hopeful of getting breakfast from the new visitors. They were making quite a racket.

Awaiting the vet inspection, Meridien paced around the airport stable, nostrils fluttering to take in the new smells. It was so cold! Charlie put Meridien's brand-new bright orange rug on him to make sure he did not get a chill. A new experience, as Meridien had not needed a rug at all in the heat of the desert.

The vet checked Meridien's passport. Over the howling and barking coming from the dogs next door, which made it hard to hear the vet as she spoke, Charlie was sure she heard the vet say that Meridien looked as if he had eaten well on the flight! Charlie chuckled to herself and smiled at Meridien, her globetrotter friend who just took every new journey in his stride.

All the necessary paperwork was signed off. Meridien had officially arrived in England. He whinnied goodbye to Whisper and Warrior and he and Charlie set off for Wiltshire.

Quarantine, Quack and Jet Lag

England

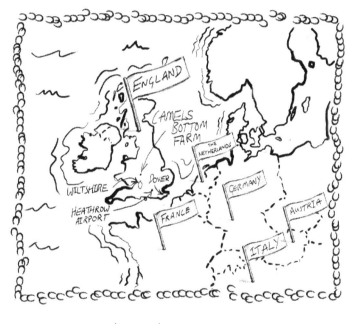

Hello! How do you do?

Meridien had to go into quarantine and isolate for six whole weeks after he arrived in England. Quarantine is part and parcel of the globetrotting life of a horse.

Whilst in isolation he was not allowed to see any other horses, but he found two friends to keep him company.

To the front of his stable was a large round pond, surrounded by reeds. The pond was home to Martin the Mallard and Douglas the Duck, both with shiny green heads and bright yellow beaks.

You might think that the two ducks would have been scared of Meridien who towered high above them. But they were not scared, and they were certainly not shy.

Every evening, as the sun set over the quarantine stables, Martin the Mallard and Douglas the Duck, seeking a warm place for the night, would waddle over to Meridien's stable and sneak in under the stable door. They would peck at any grain that Meridien had knocked onto the floor from his feed bowl and proceed to make themselves comfy in the straw that was Meridien's bed!

Globetrotting is tiring! Arriving in England from Oman, Meridien had to adjust to a new time zone - a four-hour time difference. During his first few weeks in England, Meridien was very sleepy, he was jet-lagged, and spent most of his time lying down, stretched out with Martin the Mallard and Douglas the Duck close by for company. And although his tummy would be telling him it was time for lunch, it would only just be time for breakfast. It was all rather confusing, and his tummy was grumbling all the time! He even had some meals lying down (not just breakfast in bed!) and often had to share his bowl of feed with his new friends who would quack until he let them join in the feast.

Back in the desert, each day had been divided up by the calls to prayer - chanting calls from the mosque five times a day. Now in England, for the first time

Meridien heard church bells, a ringing and dinging like the bell that rang before a jumping round at a competition. The church bells sounded much more frequently than the call to prayer: on the hour and

on the half hour. They chimed all round the clock. It was going to take some time for Meridien to get used to them and not to wake up in the middle of the night from a dream that he was competing, only to realise he was actually stretched out in a warm bed of straw in his stable, Martin the Mallard and Douglas the Duck snuggled up by his side.

Camels Bottom Farm Sweet Shop

England

From the Wiltshire quarantine stables Meridien and Charlie moved to the freedom of Camels Bottom Farm. Despite the name of the farm there were no camels' bottoms in sight - which was good, because, as Charlie experienced whilst crossing the desert, Meridien is wary of camels!

The beautiful farm in the English countryside was owned by farmer Teddy who always wore a tweed flat cap and muddy green wellies. He lived on the farm with his very talented son Eddy and his two Labradors - Ready and Steady, who roamed the farm and played with the horses whenever farmer Teddy was looking the other way.

Eddy was a very gifted rider and had been talent spotted by the head of the Queen's stables. He got to ride lots of the royal horses. Neddy was Eddy's favourite: a pretty, palomino pony who used to pull a carriage for the Queen. Now he was ridden by the talented Eddy and got to hang out in the field with Meridien in the English countryside.

Camels Bottom Farm had its own sweet shop, especially for horses. It was actually an orchard but that meant it was full of sweet treats for horses. Meridien loved the sweet shop.

Farmer Teddy had planted an orchard full of many different types of fruit trees. He spent hours pruning and tending to the trees. All his hard work paid off, and when the season was right the trees would be laden with fruit that  Meridien could sample. If an apple or a pear fell and landed close by, within Meridien's reach, it was not long before it was gobbled up!

 If only farmer Teddy could also have grown date palms - that would have been a dream come true for Meridien. But Meridien had no need to miss dates. He still had a big supply in his travelling sweet shop and once he finished those, he still did not need to worry as his friends from Abu Dhabi made sure he was never without dates. They sent frequent packages to him from the Middle East to his new home in England.

In the summer months when the cherry trees were abundant with fruit and Meridien and Charlie headed out for rides, they would take a moment and stop under the trees. Meridien

would stand quietly as Charlie manoeuvred herself so she could stand on the top of the saddle, like a trick rider, to pick cherries. Meridien came to know that if he stood quietly, Charlie would gather enough cherries to share - with him. Just like with the dates, Charlie removed the stones first.

England may not have the right climate to grow date palms, but cherries were not a bad alternative and Meridien became quite a fan!

Thanks to farmer Teddy's well-tended orchard, Meridien could add apples, pears and cherries to the mints, dates, apricots and pomegranates already stocked in his travelling sweet shop.

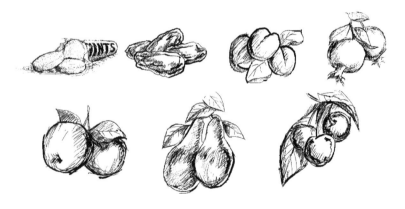

The Puddle, the Pub and the Pony

England

Charlie and Eddy became friends and would take Meridien and Neddy out for rides together.

Turning left out of Camels Bottom Farm the road led past a chicken farm. What a pong!

Further down the quiet country lane, after about five hundred metres, the road joined a pathway that ran alongside a cattle farm.

Approaching the cows for the first time, Meridien stood firm, not wanting to get any closer to the strange mooing monsters.

The cows were scary, like the monsters Hank, his tall ex-racehorse friend from Texas, had been so scared of back in Muscat - but real.

'It's OK, Meridien, I promise they are not monsters,' Charlie whispered, gently patting his neck, when suddenly, he took a leap forward and dashed past the mooing cows. Charlie clung on and just about managed not to fall off.

Past the cattle farm, Meridien alongside Neddy, Charlie and Eddy chatted.

'Look at that....' Charlie started to say, when without any warning Meridien stopped, feet stubbornly planted on the ground.

He had seen a big puddle on the path ahead. He hesitated for a moment longer, then took a step back. Not wanting to dip his twinkle toes into the murky waters, he took an enormous leap over the puddle.

Taken by surprise, Charlie flew right out of the saddle, landing in the muddy puddle with a splash.

Clear of the water, Meridien moseyed on, calm and cool as if nothing had happened, until Neddy whinnied at him from behind. He turned around only to see Charlie sat in the big puddle with mud speckled all over her face.

Meridien walked back towards Charlie and stretched his neck out to nuzzle her muddy shoulder.

'As I was about to say - look at that huge puddle!' Charlie giggled.

Eddy started laughing too, once he realised his friend was not hurt, just very grubby!

At the end of the grassy path was a beautiful, old, thatched pub with a lovely landlord called Tom who was always happy to welcome horses into his pub garden. As soon as Tom heard Meridien and Neddy *clip-clop-clip-clopping* up the road, he peered out of a window.

'Hold on, I'm on my way down!' he hollered.

By the time the horses had reached the beautiful, old, thatched pub, there waiting for Meridien and Neddy was a big red bucket full of water and a large bag of bright orange carrots.

On seeing the state of Charlie, Tom also brought a big towel so she could dry off and try to get rid of some of the mud that was absolutely everywhere!

Meridien could now add carrots to the treats stocked in his travelling sweet shop - together with his collection of mints, dates, apricots, pomegranates, apples, pears and cherries.

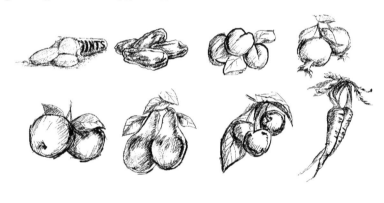

*

One day, on one of their rides, Charlie and Eddy were chatting to Tom outside the pub whilst Meridien and Neddy were playing and splashing each other with water from the big red bucket. There was a *clip-clop-clip-clopping* of another horse approaching.

Meridien and Neddy stopped their antics and pricked their ears in the direction of the hoof beats.

Headed towards the pub was a young lady riding a cheeky looking chestnut mare with a white blaze - like Meridien's, just a bit broader. None of them recognised the pony or the rider.

'Bring your pony over for some water and carrots,' Tom called out to the young lady. 'Come join us!'

Smiling at Tom, the rider said, 'Serenade would love to, thank you!'

Charlie and Eddy welcomed the young lady, patting Serenade on the neck as she came over to join them.

'Hi, I'm Judy. My parents have just bought the pub in the next village. Serenade - my cheeky pony - and I were out exploring the area for the first time.'

'Eddy and Neddy know all the best places to ride round here and Meridien and I love to go exploring. We will show you and Serenade around,' Charlie told Judy excitedly.

Charlie, Eddy and Judy became great friends.

Every weekend they would head off on rides in the countryside together. Their laughter could be heard echoing across the hills as they told each other funny stories.

Without fail they would always stop by to see Tom. A big red bucket full of water and a large bag of bright orange carrots would be waiting for the horses in the pub garden.

Tom was always happy to see them all but would give Judy an especially big smile - and a slice of her favourite cake that he made for her every weekend.

*

Thousands of miles away from the desert, Meridien and Charlie had quickly found a very happy new life in the English countryside with fabulous friends. The lush green of the countryside was such a contrast to the reds and yellows of the sandy desert. Both were beautiful, both so very different.

Variety is the spice of life! Although Meridien would probably say that dates, and maybe carrots, are the spice of life!

All Aboard!

England and the Sea

Ahoy!
(An English greeting used at sea)

Change was in the air again. The HUGE green suitcase was packed. Meridien was headed away from England's sweet shop orchards, rolling green hills and pubs with friendly landlords. Meridien was off on another globe trot and this trip was an epic journey in itself.

England is part of Great Britain, an island. To get off an island, usually, there are three options: to fly, to swim or to sail. Meridien had flown to England on a plane. He was certainly not going to swim! He was to set sail.

'Safe journey my duck,' said farmer Teddy, in his friendly country accent, as he hugged Charlie goodbye. 'Be sure to come back soon.'

Eddy waved from the window of the farmhouse, sad to see his good friends leaving.

Meridien and the HUGE green suitcase were loaded up into the horsebox and they set off.

As they travelled away from Camels Bottom Farm, for three long hours Meridien munched hay. Then they came to a stop. The horsebox was stationary, parked up for a long time.

After a few hours Charlie opened the ramp and took Meridien out of the horsebox and for a walk around a big car park. There were lots of lorries and cars. People were honking their horns, making quite a din. The rain was lashing down. Beyond the car park, where the land met the sea, ferries were bobbing up and down, swaying from side to side - a strange new sight for Meridien.

Back up onto the horsebox and they were off again - for another three hours of munching hay. Eventually the horsebox slowed down and came to a stop. The moment when Meridien's new destination would be revealed had arrived. The ramp opened. There was barking. It sounded like Ready and Steady. There was a loud whinny. It sounded just like Neddy. Was that Camels Bottom Farm again? It looked very similar and the smells were familiar. Was there another place six hours away that looked exactly the same? A place that had the same smells?

As Meridien walked off the horsebox, Ready and Steady ran to greet him. Neddy cantered over to the gate of his field to see what was going on and to whinny to his friend.

'You're back!' shouted Eddy, smiling and dashing out of the house to welcome his friends back home.

They were back at Camels Bottom Farm. That was a strange journey!

Later that week there was another three-hour journey to a car park for a walk in the rain and then back home to Camels Bottom Farm - all very confusing.

The weather had been so bad that each time they arrived at the ferry port in Dover the ferry was cancelled due to big storms and choppy waters. No boats had been allowed to set sail.

The day of the third attempt the skies were clear and there was not even a breeze to rustle the leaves on the cherry trees. Farmer Teddy and Eddy, standing with Neddy, waved goodbye to Meridien and Charlie again, Eddy secretly hoping his friends would be back again in a few hours. But this time, there was no stop for a walk around the car park and Meridien's journey continued in a way that he had never experienced before.

Meridien had his hay net taken away. What was that all about? He was not impressed. The horsebox

was not moving but he was. It was a new sensation, a sort of floating feeling. Meridien had become very used to flying on planes and the strange tipping of the flying horsebox for take-off and landing. The ferry was different. He was floating, his legs felt wobbly. He was hungry. The air smelt very different:

heavy and salty. Sailing was a new experience. Not bad, just an unknown.

Before long, the horsebox was back on the road, back on solid ground. His legs felt more stable. This he was used to, and it was not long before he got his hay back. All was well in the world.

They passed through France, the country of his birth. His first time back there for many, many years - but there was no time to stop and visit.

It was night-time when the horsebox slowed down and stopped again. They had arrived. Charlie opened the ramp and Meridien peeked outside. There was a big canal just to the right. As Charlie walked Meridien down the ramp, he whinnied loudly, calling out in the hope of hearing Neddy's familiar greeting - but they were not back at Camels Bottom Farm. The only response was a loud quacking. Meridien's whinny had awoken a paddling of ducks from their sleep as they floated along the canal. It was not Martin the Mallard or Douglas the Duck. These were much bigger ducks whose white feathers glinted in the moonlight, as they splashed and quacked in surprise.

Meridien had arrived at his new home amongst the canals and windmills of Amsterdam - in the Netherlands.

Bad Hair Day

The Netherlands

Hoi!
(Dutch for 'Hi!')

The winters in Amsterdam were cold and wet. Charlie had built up quite a collection of horse rugs to keep Meridien warm as the winds blew and the snows came. Meridien also had his own way of keeping warm: as the winter came, his coat would change from sleek and shiny to soft and fluffy. He grew his own winter coat - mother nature's way of making sure he never gets cold.

'Right Meridien, as much as I love your fluffy coat, it's time for a clip again. You are just getting too hot and sweaty after jumping practice. I don't want you to catch a chill,' Charlie said to Meridien as she led him out of his stable one morning.

Charlie went to turn on the clippers to start shaving off Meridien's fluffy coat. They sounded like a noisy lawnmower and they tickled Meridien, especially on his tummy.

'Please be a good boy, Meridien,' Charlie pleaded, knowing that Meridien was not a big fan of the clippers.

She started clipping but after she had clipped just part of one side of Meridien's body, he started to dance and prance as he had learnt from watching the moves of his Arabian friends back in the desert. He danced and pranced so much that Charlie could not keep close by his side and tickle him with the clippers.

'Will you just stand still!' Charlie said firmly to Meridien, feeling a little frustrated.

She hopped and skipped around to avoid Meridien landing on her toes.

'Fine, we will stop for today. I think that will be safer for both of us!' Charlie said to Meridien as she turned off the clippers.

The tickling stopped and Meridien was calm again.

'But you do look a little odd with part of your fluffy coat left on!' Charlie muttered under her breath.

The following morning Charlie rode Meridien in the big indoor arena. They were practising dressage moves in front of the mirror. It was very handy to practise this horse ballet in front of the mirror, so that Charlie, and Meridien if he was paying attention, could see if they were getting the moves right. Meridien was paying attention that day. He caught a glimpse of himself in the mirror and from a canter he jolted to a halt. Charlie clung on and just managed to stay in the saddle. He had seen his unfinished haircut and was clearly not impressed.

Charlie laughed, 'I did warn you Meridien! I promise we will find a way to fix it tomorrow.'

The next day Charlie went up to Meridien in his stable. 'We really do need to fix this terrible haircut today Meridien. But don't worry. I have an idea.'

Before they had left the Middle East, the kind Argentinian vet had given Charlie some of the

delicious date-flavoured medicine and told her that she could use it if Meridien ever got scared and needed calming down.

She dug around in the HUGE green suitcase and pulled out the bottle of the special medicine, pouring a small amount into her hand.

'Look Meridien, it's your favourite medicine,' she said, holding out her hand towards him.

Meridien bobbed his head up and down as soon as the sweet smell wafted in his direction. He stretched his neck out to reach to Charlie's hand and in flash he had eaten it all up.

The kind Argentinian vet was right, it had an almost magical effect and although Meridien could still hear the nasty tickling machine, it did not seem to bother him anymore.

Charlie fixed the terrible, unfinished, embarrassing haircut. Meridien was all smart again.

Sophie

The Netherlands

It was in Amsterdam that Meridien met Sophie.

Sophie cycled past the stables every day after school.

In the Netherlands everybody cycles. There are more bicycles than people. Sophie liked to cycle, but she really wanted to ride a horse. She wanted to ride Meridien, the big orange horse with the big white blaze (it cannot be denied that when the sun shines on Meridien's golden coat, he is a very bright orange). She had seen him out in the field by the canal every day when she cycled past. She always stopped and gave him a pat on the neck and a rub on his forehead. Meridien came to expect Sophie's visits.

Orange was Sophie's favourite colour, and she always wore something orange. It was the colour of Meridien and the colour of her royal family, the House of Orange. Sophie wanted to be a princess when she grew up, a princess of the House of Orange.

In the Netherlands, every year there is a big party on the King's birthday and the whole country takes the day off. It is called King's Day. As part of the festivities there is a special procession in The Hague, the home of the House of Orange. Sophie's school had a King's Day competition that year. The pupil who came up with the best and most unique way to represent the House of Orange could go to the King's birthday party and take part in the procession. The princesses of the House of Orange and royalty from all over Europe would be there.

Sophie had an idea and was convinced that she could win the competition.

Cycling home from school that day she was rehearsing the speech she had prepared to give at the stables. She knew what she needed to say. She just needed to find the right person to speak to.

She was extremely nervous, but she was going to be brave.

Sophie stopped at the side of Meridien's field and hopped off her bicycle. She gave him a scratch on the forehead. 'Wish me luck!' she whispered.

She picked up her bicycle that she had laid down on the grass and Meridien turned and watched as Sophie walked down towards the stables for the first time.

Walking towards the paddock to the side of the stables, Charlie called in a shrill voice. 'Meridien, Meridien, come here boy!'
He came trotting towards her and up to the gate.

Almost at the gate, Charlie was ready to catch Meridien who was whinnying softly to her. Then, out of the corner of her eye Charlie saw a girl with curly blond locks. She did not recognise the girl.

'Can I help you?' Charlie asked.

'My name is Sophie. I'm looking for the owner of this beautiful orange horse. He's so friendly. I wanted to ask if I could take him to the King's Day procession. It's for a competition at school. I thought it would be great to take an orange horse to represent the House of Orange!' Sophie told Charlie, speaking at a hundred miles an hour.

Charlie smiled. She walked up to Meridien and beckoned to Sophie to follow her.

'Well, Sophie: You have found the right person to ask,' Charlie told the little girl with curly blond locks. 'And of course, it would be fantastic for Meridien to show off his best orange to the House of Orange. I love the idea!'

'That's amazing, thank you so, so much,' replied Sophie. 'Now I have to tell my teachers, but I am sure that riding an orange horse in the procession for the King of Orange on his birthday will be the best and most unique idea. I'm sure we

will win the competition. I'll come back tomorrow after school and let you know.'

The next day at school Sophie told her teachers her idea and, at the end of classes that day, Sophie was announced the winner. She jumped on her bicycle and pedalled as fast as she could to the stables.

Charlie was grooming Meridien when she saw Sophie flying down the lane towards her.

'Does this mean we can go to the party?' she asked Sophie as she approached.

'Yes! We won!' said Sophie, leaning her bicycle against the paddock fence and skipping over to Meridien and Charlie.

They laughed excitedly as they fussed over Meridien. Charlie promised that Sophie could ride him one day, but there was not time for her to learn before King's Day which was just a few weeks away. It was agreed: Charlie would ride Meridien at the King's Day procession and Sophie could walk proudly by Meridien's side.

On the day of the procession Sophie arrived early in the morning to help get Meridien ready. She helped Charlie wash and groom and polish and shine. Meridien looked fit for a King. He needed to be as he was off to meet the King of Orange!

They travelled to The Hague in the horsebox. On the journey Charlie told Sophie some of the tales of Meridien's travels around the globe. She also told her about his love of treats, his travelling sweet shop and how dates were his absolute favourite food.

The procession took place in the big square in front of the palace, the home of the King. It was a big party. There was a band playing. Everybody was wearing orange. Even the dogs people had brought with them to the party were wearing a varied selection of orange collars, bows and ribbons. But Meridien was the only horse. Sophie's idea really was unique.

This would be a day that Sophie would never forget. It was magical. She saw all the royal family and all the princesses, all of their tiaras and all of their shiny jewels. She knew she was so lucky to be there. And it was her bright thinking and Meridien that had made it possible.

The King of Orange, who was wearing a bright orange tie, went round shaking hands with people. Then he went up to Meridien. He reached into his pocket and pulled out an orange (what else!).

'May I give this beautiful orange horse an orange?' asked the King.

'Happy Birthday, Your Majesty, and of course,' replied Charlie politely.

'I'm sure Meridien will like the orange,' said Sophie confidently as she looked up at the King of Orange. 'But he prefers dates. Dates from Abu Dhabi!'

The King of Orange laughed and thanked Sophie for the special information.

Meridien still got his orange and nodded in appreciation at this new treat. Oranges would definitely be added to his travelling sweet shop!

Meridien's travelling sweet shop was now stocked with mints, dates, apricots, pomegranates, apples, pears, cherries, carrots and oranges.

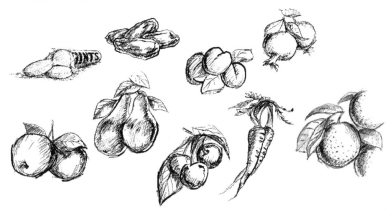

In addition to the orange Meridien was given a special thank you gift from the House of Orange - a thank you to the French horse who had come to join in their celebrations. It was a brand-new rug. The design on the rug was an airmail letter with a big Dutch flag on it, very appropriate for a globetrotter. From that day on, the Dutch airmail rug travelled with Meridien in his HUGE green suitcase on all of his journeys.

Meridien left the Netherlands a few months after King's Day, but Charlie made sure Sophie had the chance to ride him many times before they headed off on their next journey.

To this day Sophie still writes letters to Meridien. Letters always sent by airmail.

More Sweet Treats and the Sound of Music

Austria

Grüß Gott!
(you say 'Groose Gott' –
a typical Austrian greeting)

After a long journey in the horsebox from Amsterdam by road, not by sea on the wobbly floaty boat this time, Meridien and Charlie arrived in Vienna, the capital city of Austria. Meridien's new home was on the edge of the famous Viennese forest.

Once settled in, Charlie and Meridien would go for long rides through the forest and the fields close by. The terrain was new for both of them. They would trot through tall fields of sweetcorn plants. Meridien was very tall himself but the plants were taller and no matter how hard he tried he could not peek over the top. They would wind their way up and down the narrow paths between the plants - it was like being in a maze! Charlie would pick corn on the cob and stuff it into her pockets. Once out of the plant  maze, knowing Charlie would always take some corn on the cob for him from the fields, Meridien would jog home in anticipation of munching on the sweet yellow treat.

The other horses at the stables in Vienna would chomp on another long, yellow, sweet treat - bananas! Meridien, always open to sampling new treats, tried a banana but just spat it right out! So, his travelling sweet shop was now stocked with

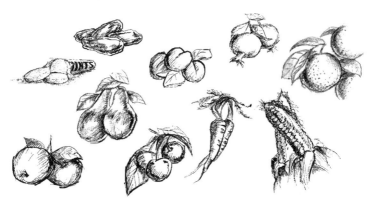

mints, dates, apricots, pomegranates, apples, pears, cherries, carrots, oranges and corn on the cob - but not bananas.

Bright and early one morning Meridien and Charlie rode up into the hills and deep into the thick forest behind Vienna. Trotting along boldly, Meridien's ears pricked up.

'You can hear the music too, huh,' Charlie said to Meridien. 'Let's find out where it is coming from.'

They followed the sound of the music. It grew louder and Meridien started to jog and bounce along.

'Do you think it's a competition? Is that why you are suddenly so excited?' Charlie said, laughing at Meridien's sudden enthusiasm.

They followed the winding track until they reached a clearing in the forest. The place was bustling with people. At the centre of the crowd was a big brass band playing the music they had heard from the distance. There were shiny instruments of all different sizes glinting in the sunlight that shone through into the glade. It was an oompah band: *oom-pah-oom-pah-oom-pah-pah!* Men dressed in traditional lederhosen and ladies in traditional dirndls were laughing and dancing. Meridien joined in and was  also jigging along to the sound of the Austrian music. What a cultural tour of the world he was getting!

Meridien started to whinny as two horses came prancing towards the crowd from the other side of the clearing. It was Yin and Yang. Yin who was black as the night and Yang who was white as snow - the two American trick horses who were at Meridien's stables in Muscat. They whinnied back to Meridien recognising him and his whinny straight away.

The crowd moved to one side, alongside the oompah band, making space for the horses. Yin and Yang started to perform to the music: *oom-pah-oom-pah-oom-pah-pah!*

Riders dressed in sparkly and spangly outfits ran out from behind the crowd and leapt up onto the horses as they cantered round in circles in time to the rhythm of the music and in perfect harmony with each other.

An announcement came through a loudspeaker: 'Please put your hands together to welcome the talented and daring twins from Muscat - Mo and Meriem!'

It was little Lina's twin brother and sister!

The captivated onlookers started clapping and cheering, then gasping as the besequinned Mo and Meriem performed handstands, back flips, and all sorts of spectacular moves on top of the cantering horses.

As Meridien and Charlie stood by and watched, a young Austrian boy in lederhosen came running over.

'I am Hans,' he said. 'Are you and your beautiful horse with the big white blaze also going to perform some tricks?' he asked Charlie.

Charlie laughed.

'Not today!' she replied. 'We were just out exploring in the forest and followed the sound of the music. Meridien is a show jumper, not a trick horse like Yin and Yang over there.'

Hans stayed with Meridien and Charlie as they watched the acrobatics and he made a fuss of Meridien, rubbing his neck, and giving him a good scratch. Meridien was enjoying the attention and nuzzled Hans's shoulder as a sign of appreciation.

Once Yin, Yang, Mo and Meriem had finished their performance, Hans turned to Charlie and asked how to spell Meridien's name. Charlie told him and then he dashed away.

Charlie led Meridien over to their old friends from Oman. They were equally surprised and elated to meet her and Meridien there in the middle of the Viennese forest, far away from where they had last seen each other in Muscat.

'Is little Lina with you?' Charlie asked Mo and Meriem, excited at the thought of meeting up with her close friend and maybe sharing some more riding adventures together.

'No, she's gone to America to train to be a jockey, but let's take a selfie to send to her. I know she would have been so happy to see you,' replied Mo, who reached for his phone and stretched out his arm as far as he could to make sure Meridien, Yin and Yang were in the photo too.

'Text her that we will visit her one day,' Charlie told the twins, glancing across to Meridien as she plotted another journey in her head.

Hans came running back towards them, carrying something in his hand. Grinning, he held it up for all to see - a big traditional ginger-spiced, iced biscuit in the shape of a heart.

The letters M-E-R-I-D-I-E-N were written  across the middle in bright orange icing - bright orange just like Meridien!

Hans was so happy to be offering this traditional souvenir to Meridien that he did not notice Meridien sniffing at the biscuit and proceeding to take a big, tasty bite! Meridien nodded his head in appreciation, so Hans, laughing, let him eat the whole thing. Charlie was laughing too as it was typical of Meridien to want to try a new treat.

With the special souvenir biscuit all gobbled up, Charlie waved goodbye to Mo, Meriem and Hans and they headed back onto the forest track and set off for home. Meridien whinnied farewell to his trick horse friends Yin and Yang.

As much as Meridien had enjoyed this new treat, Charlie did not want him eating human biscuits all the time, so they were kept as a munch memory and not added to the travelling sweet shop!

Roaring and Snoring

Austria

In every new country that Meridien was lucky enough to visit and explore, there were always lots of new sounds, some fun, some scary. In Abu Dhabi there was the call to prayer, in England there were the church bells and the scary mooing cows. Everywhere he went there always seemed to be something he heard for the first time.

In Austria, the sound of the oompah band in the forest had been fun and reminded him of the music he enjoyed at competitions.

But there were frightening sounds in Austria too. The village next to his stables would test the sound system for the warning siren once a month on a Saturday morning in case they ever needed to alert the villagers in an emergency. It started out like the call to prayer: a gentle wailing. But the sound grew louder and shrill. Meridien would pace around his stable restlessly whilst the alarm was sounding. Once it was over and it was quiet again, he would settle back down and return to munching his hay. Fortunately, it did not happen five times a day like the call to prayer or on the hour and every half hour like the church bells!

Then there were the sounds of the night, scary sounds of the night. Meridien always lies down to sleep at night. He likes to get comfortable for his slumber. His new friend Otto the stable cat curled up with him in the straw, sometimes he would be awoken, suddenly. Woken up by a large BANG, then a FLASH. Otto would flee, startled, and Meridien would jump to his feet. It was as if someone had put the lights on and off. BANG again! CRASH! A roar? Were there mountain lions in Vienna? All the horses were startled, eyes on stalks, senses heightened, dashing around restlessly in their stables. Sometimes the banging and flashing lasted for hours and hours. Meridien could not sleep through the noise and the commotion, whatever it was.

But it was not a pride of roaring mountain lions roaming outside the stables, it was just a thunderstorm. Meridien had never experienced anything like it. The unknown was frightening, but once it was over, he would lie back down, his fear forgotten. Otto the stable cat (definitely a cat and not a mountain lion!) would join him again and they would curl up and go back to sleep. A sound like thunder was still roaring, just more quietly, almost softly. That was Meridien snoring! Meridien always snores in his sleep. However, the gentle roar of Meridien's snore did not keep the other horses awake, and it lulled Otto the stable cat into a deep, dreamy sleep.

Magic Powers?

Germany

Guten Tag!
(German for 'Hello!' or 'Good Day!')

Another journey by road in the horsebox took them to Germany. They arrived in Heidelberg, the beautiful university city on the river Neckar. With its magnificent castle nestled on the hill that overlooks the medieval town below, this city full of tradition and history was Meridien's new home.

For the first time ever, Meridien had a stable with its own private garden. He could let himself in and out whenever he pleased. It was a real luxury.

As always, Meridien made new friends quickly. His best friend in Heidelberg was a tall, bay ex-racehorse with a gleaming, black mane and tail. His name was Ticket, and he was from Ireland. Ticket and Meridien could see into each other's neighbouring stables and they would meet outside and groom each other and play across the fence in their own little private gardens.

Once the hot summer had turned into autumn and it grew colder, Meridien noticed Charlie with a stepladder and a toolbox in his stable.

'Careful! Stand back Meridien! I need to hang up this curtain between your stable and your garden. It will stop the cold wind and the snow blowing in,' Charlie explained to Meridien.

Meridien kept away from the banging and hammering noises that Charlie was making from the top of the stepladder as she hung up the clear plastic curtain.

'Ticket has one too. Just watch how he still goes in and out. Good boy!' she said as she left Meridien to investigate the new curtain.

Indeed, Ticket continued to go in and out from his stable to the garden and back. Only Meridien could not get to him when he was outside. Meridien was stuck inside behind the curtain. He paced up and down in his stable, frustrated. He wanted to play outside with Ticket. But he could no longer get outside. He could not get through the curtain. Or could he?

He stood and looked on as Ticket walked straight through the curtain. Was it magic?

Some nights, when the moon was full, Meridien had seen a little girl wearing a pink cape and a carrying a silver wand drift silently into the stables and sprinkle fairy dust over some of the horses. Once she had sprinkled the fairy dust she would disappear into the moonlight without a trace. Meridien had never noticed any of the fairy dust reach him in his stable but he had seen Ticket be showered with the sparkly fairy dust. Maybe it gave Ticket magic powers to be able to walk through the curtain?

Did Meridien need the fairy dust to have magic powers? He could sort of see through the curtain and he could just about poke his nose out. But how was Ticket walking through it? He pushed the curtain with his nose. It fell back on him, surprised him. He jumped away. Eager to be outside with Ticket, he poked at the curtain again, with more force this time. The curtain bounced back even harder against his nose. It was frustrating!

Then, Meridien suddenly took a huge leap. An actual leap and a leap of faith.

Ticket was startled as his friend burst through the curtain, squealing as he flew into the garden!

Maybe he did have magic powers after all! Maybe Meridien did not need the fairy dust like the other horses.

Forever Friends

Germany

Most mornings, there would be a girl, Johanna, sitting in the corner of Ticket's stable. She would sit there polishing her saddle and talking to Ticket. Of course, she also talked to  Meridien now that he had moved in next door. Charlie and Johanna became friends, and they would go out on rides together with Meridien and Ticket along the river and across the fields behind the city. There were big fields of corn on the cob, like in Vienna. So Meridien's travelling sweet shop was kept well stocked with corn on the cob!

One morning, very early, the girls set out on a ride with Meridien and Ticket and turned right. Not left. They usually went left. The horses both jogged along, eager to explore the new route. It was the path that headed along the river towards the castle.

As it was still very early, there were not many people about: just a few dog walkers and a handful of joggers. Meridien and Ticket had the river path almost to themselves.

Where the riverbank grew wide, the two horses raced alongside each other playfully. Enjoying the experience of discovering a new place, they snorted with excitement and fluttered their nostrils to take in all the new smells. The closer they got to town, the bigger the castle appeared, perched up on the hillside. Then the path grew narrow again. The water from the river lapped up onto what became a towpath. Meridien still did not like to get his feet wet. He did not want to dip his twinkle toes into the water and jumped all the puddles.

They rode as far as the beautiful medieval bridge which they started to cross to join the road that led up to the castle. *Clip-clop-clip-clopping* along they trotted over the bridge. Suddenly Meridien flinched. Something was not right. Charlie gasped, short of breath. She fell forward onto Meridien's neck, her arms dropped to the sides. Meridien very gently slowed down to a walk, Ticket right by his side.

Johanna saw Charlie slumped on Meridien's neck and screamed at the top of her voice. 'My friend is poorly! Help! Come and help Charlie!'

The horses came to a halt. Meridien craned his neck to turn and nudge Charlie, but she did not react.

A tall young man came running over. Meridien did not stir. The man slid Charlie off Meridien's back and lifted her to the ground. She was not breathing. Meridien whinnied, fluttering his nostrils and calling to her. The man tried to resuscitate Charlie as Johanna and the horses looked on, distraught.

The wailing siren of an ambulance could be heard in the distance. It was getting louder. It was coming closer. Johanna had called the ambulance as soon as she could and it was already turning onto the bridge, blue lights flashing.

Meridien whinnied again, a distressed whinny, not his usual soft whinny. Within a matter of minutes, the paramedics took Charlie away to the ambulance.

Johanna was in shock, worried about Charlie, plus she had a problem and was thinking about how to solve it: she had to get both horses safely back to the stables. The river path was narrow, too narrow for two horses, side by side.

'Johanna, what happened? Are you OK?' shouted a familiar voice.

It was Laura, Johanna and Charlie's friend from the stables.

'I was out on my morning run along the river. I saw the horses on the bridge and heard the ambulance. Where is Charlie?' asked Laura, concerned.

Johanna had never been so happy to see Laura, a friend who was there when she needed her most.

'Can you help me get the horses home safely?' Johanna asked her friend. 'I will tell you what happened on the way.'

Without hesitation Laura took Meridien by the reins and jumped up into the saddle.

The two worried friends and the two unsettled horses headed back along the river to the stables, as fast as they could. As they rode along, Johanna recounted the events of the morning to Laura and explained that Charlie had been taken by ambulance to hospital.

Once they got back to the stables, Laura took care of Meridien and Ticket and Johanna hurried to the hospital. The doctors told her Charlie was in good hands, and they would call her when she was ready for visitors.

It was a few days after the incident on the bridge before Charlie woke up. Slowly, she opened her eyes. She was confused. She did not recognise her surroundings. Everything was white and clinical and there was a strong smell of disinfectant.

She overheard a voice in the corridor.

'Room 11. This is Charlie. She came in by ambulance five days ago. Her heart stopped whilst she was riding her horse and a stranger came quickly to her rescue. She's a very luck girl,' she heard the voice say from outside in the corridor.

Charlie did not remember the stranger. In fact, she did not remember much.

'How is she doing now?' Charlie heard a different voice ask.

'Well, very well. She has just woken up from a deep sleep and her heart is working normally again,' said the first voice.

'Shall we go in and see the patient?' the first voice asked.

There was a knock at the door and two doctors in white coats approached Charlie's hospital bed.

'I'm Doctor Heart and this is my colleague Doctor Beat, how are you feeling?'

Charlie was very tired, too tired to speak, so she just blinked her eyes and tried her best to smile at the doctors.

'Rest up Charlie, you are doing well. We will be back to check on you later,' Doctor Heart said, and they both left again, closing the door to her hospital room behind them.

After Doctor Heart and Doctor Beat left, Charlie dozed off to sleep again. When she woke up, she still felt weak but had just enough strength to turn her head towards the light which was shining through a window into her hospital room. Was she dreaming? Was that Meridien outside the window? With Ticket?

Then she heard a voice calling her name from outside the window.

She recognised that voice. It was the loud voice that had screamed for help on the beautiful old bridge. It all came flooding back to her - it was Johanna, her friend with the loud voice that had saved her life.

Johanna had pleaded with Doctor Heart and Doctor Beat to be there when Charlie woke up. Not just her, but to be there with the horses. She knew that would be the best medicine for Charlie for a speedy recovery. She also knew she could rely on Laura to help ride the horses to the hospital.

Johanna pushed open the window from the outside. The two horses were curious and poked their noses towards the window. Meridien and Ticket both gave off a low soft whinny. The sound reached Charlie in her hospital bed and a huge smile spread across her face.

After that first visit, every day Charlie waited for the *clip-clop-clip-clopping* in the distance. She

would hear the horses trotting up the road until they stopped at the window of her hospital room to wish her well. Laura would ride Meridien, and Johanna would ride Ticket.

Soon Charlie was well again, well enough to leave the hospital. Soon, well enough to get back into the saddle. All thanks to the doctors and nurses and amazing friends of the two legged and four-legged kind who had looked out for her.

Heidelberg will always have a special place in Charlie's heart and Meridien's too. A place of friendship bonds they will never forget.

*

Charlie was sad when they eventually had to leave Heidelberg, but the HUGE green suitcase was packed, and she and Meridien were off again on another journey.

'Don't be a stranger,' Johanna said to Charlie, as she hugged her goodbye.

'We will all miss you and Meridien so much,' added Laura. 'And please take good care of yourself.'

'We are only going to England this time. It's not that far away. You should come visit us at Camels

Bottom Farm,' Charlie told her friends. 'Meridien and I will be waiting for you!'

'We will, we will!' Johanna and Laura chanted.

'I'm not sure how I can ever thank you enough, but thank you, thank you, thank you,' Charlie told the girls as she gave them both a big bear hug.

Meridien and Ticket whinnied to each other as Meridien and Charlie set off on their journey to the North, back to England on the ferry. There were no storms this time and it was plain sailing all the way to Dover.

They returned to the familiar surroundings of Camels Bottom Farm, back to see farmer Teddy, his son and Charlie's friend Eddy, Eddy's horse Neddy and the two Labradors Ready and Steady.

The Hospital

England

Hello again!

One cold spring morning back at Camels Bottom Farm, despite the frost in the air, Meridien was hot. Very hot and sweaty. He was not himself. In his stable he was restless. He had a big net of hay, but he did not touch it. Something in his tummy was causing him pain. He moved around, trying to run away from it, whatever it was. It would not go away, no matter how he stretched and strained. If only the little girl wearing a pink cape and carrying a silver wand from Heidelberg would come to his rescue with some fairy dust and give him magic powers to make him feel better. The kind Argentinian vet with the delicious date-flavoured medicine who had always made him feel better would also have been a very welcome visitor that morning. But neither of them appeared.

Ready and Steady had slept in their usual spot on the straw bales just outside Meridien's stable and were awoken by his groaning and flustered frolicking around the stable. Sensing something was wrong, they started barking. Ready ran off to the farmhouse. Steady stayed with Meridien, growling softly at him, confused and worried by his new behaviour - Meridien was normally so calm.

Ready came running back into the stable yard, followed by farmer Teddy and Eddy. Charlie was a few paces behind, still in her pyjamas. One glance at Meridien and it was clear to them that there was a problem. Meridien looked unsettled. He was off his food - for the first time ever. He had lost his sheen and his sparkle. His shimmering chestnut coat was dulled, the orange gleam had faded.

Flustered and upset, Charlie, phone in hand, was already talking to the vet. Not the kind Argentinian vet, as he was thousands of miles away, back in Abu Dhabi, but Emma, Meridien's favourite English vet. Emma was a big fan of Meridien and when she heard he was unwell, she dashed to the stables as fast as humanly possible, possibly even faster.

When Emma arrived at the stables, Charlie was walking Meridien around outside to try and help ease his tummy pain. He looked so sad. Charlie had

never seen him so sad. She never wanted to see him that sad again.

Emma explained calmly to Charlie, 'We need to get Meridien to the horse hospital as quickly as possible.'

'Will he be OK?' Charlie asked nervously, stroking Meridien's neck to try and comfort him.

'He has a nasty bout of colic and we just need to make sure it doesn't get any worse and cause long term damage to his intestine,' Emma said. 'I'll give him something to ease the pain and discomfort for the journey. That should help.'

It was not as good as the delicious date-flavoured medicine that the kind Argentinian vet gave him back in Abu Dhabi, but it did make him feel better. It was not the moment for eating dates anyway.

Ready and Steady barked non-stop as Charlie loaded Meridien up onto the horsebox. Eddy tried to calm the dogs down, but as the horsebox headed off, they pulled away from him and chased behind, following Meridien. Farmer Teddy was at the bottom of the lane and managed to stop Ready and Steady in their pursuit of the horsebox.

With one hand farmer Teddy waved Meridien off on his journey to the horse hospital in

Newmarket, and with the other he patted his trusty Labradors.

'Well done for alerting us that Meridien was poorly - you clever dogs! And don't worry, the vets will do everything they can to make Meridien better,' Farmer Teddy said reassuringly to Ready and Steady.

Meridien and Charlie had been on much longer journeys but, worried about Meridien, the journey felt to Charlie as if it went on forever.

They arrived at the horse hospital. It was shiny and new. There was a strong smell that made Meridien's nostrils flare. It was disinfectant, bringing back memories of the hospital in Heidelberg where Charlie had been taken after her heart stopped beating. There were rows of big, whitewashed stables and lots of other buildings dotted around: operating theatres, treatment rooms, a dedicated space for physiotherapy and even a swimming pool for horses. It was palatial, similar to the palaces Meridien and Charlie had seen in Abu Dhabi and Oman. Hopefully, the familiarity made Meridien feel more at ease. Even in his poorly state.

Meridien was taken to a stable that had been prepared for his arrival. He had not had a drink for a while - and it really is true that you can take a horse to water, but you cannot make it drink - so to make sure he had enough fluids in his body, he was put on a drip: a big bag of goodness suspended from the very high ceiling of the stable and attached to his neck by a long spirally cable.

Even with this contraption attached, Meridien was still able to walk around his stable freely whilst the goodness worked its way down through the long spirally cable into his body and to his tummy. He started to feel better, much better. The ache was going away. Meridien had not received a visit from either the little girl wearing a pink cape and carrying a silver wand or the kind Argentinian vet with the delicious date medicine - maybe the goodness in the big bag hanging over his head had magic powers too.

The hospital vets and veterinary nurses who looked after him were amazing and so kind. Monitoring him carefully, they made sure he was comfortable and free of pain. They groomed him and fussed over him. Meridien was a good patient - a patient patient - and he loved all the attention.

Gradually he could start eating again - a handful of grass a few times a day. Not what he was used to, but enough for now. He would not be tucking into the treats from his travelling sweet shop for a little while yet.

He started going out for little walks, each day going a little further. He was much stronger already.

Seven days after Meridien had arrived in hospital, Emma announced, with a big smile, that he could go home.

'He'll be back to eating dates again very soon!' she jested.

'What a relief! Thank you so much Emma,' Charlie replied.

Poor Meridien had had a tough week, but he was on the mend.

Back home at Camels Bottom Farm, Charlie sat on the floor in the corner of Meridien's stable, watching him as he snoozed.

'You do not know how worried I have been. I will not be letting you out of my sight from now on!' Charlie told her four-legged, globetrotting friend.

Meridien nuzzled Charlie's shoulder and she gave him a big hug.

All is well that ends well.

Thanks to Ready and Steady for noticing that Meridien was unwell, to Charlie and Emma's quick action to get him to the hospital and the hospital vets working their own special magic, Meridien was going to be just fine.

Get Me to the Church On Time!

England

Back home at Camels Bottom Farm, Meridien was his old self again: munching hay and demanding dates. Both his and Charlie's hospital visits were long forgotten.

The horsebox pulled up, engine rumbling, at the ready for another journey. Meridien was looking especially dapper. All plaited up with white ribbons in his tail.

He had never had ribbons in his tail before.

Where was he off to now?

He bounded up the ramp of the horsebox. No friends joined him on the journey. But his HUGE green suitcase stayed behind at the stables. That meant they could not be going far.

After a short journey, the ramp opened. The horsebox was parked up just outside a pub. It was not the pub Meridien knew, with the lovely landlord Tom. It was the pub owned by Judy's parents where she kept Serenade in a field just down the lane. It was set at the foot of the hills by a stony track leading up to some woods. It was a beautiful English summer's day and there were people sitting around the picnic tables laid out on the lawn to the front, laughing and chatting.

There was a *clip-clop-clip-clopping* coming up the road. Meridien recognised the hoof beats. It was Serenade, the cheeky chestnut mare with a white blaze - Judy's pony. She was also all stylish with plaits and white ribbons. All dressed up just to go to the pub?

Charlie called out excitedly to Eddy who was riding Serenade. Judy was busy - she was getting married that afternoon! Charlie and Eddy had planned to surprise Judy at her wedding and Eddy had secretly arranged to bring Serenade along. Riding Meridien and Serenade, Charlie and Eddy were going to meet Judy outside the marquee at the wedding reception. They could not wait to see the smile on Judy's face when she saw her favourite four-legged friends there with her on her special day.

With some time to spare before the wedding reception, Charlie and Eddy decided to go on a short ride up the stony track and into the woods. They headed off, leaving the pub behind them. The people sitting at the picnic tables looked up, distracted from their conversations, and watched as the two smart riders on two smart horses trotted off.

Meridien knew to come back to a walk before the sharp bend in the track. Serenade knew she was meant to slow down too, but, cheeky and naughty as ever, she just carried on at a fast trot. Too fast!

Eddy, not used to riding naughty ponies, was holding on - just. Then, Serenade decided it was her moment for some fun. Hardly past the corner, she bolted. A flat out gallop up the hill and a little buck of joy.

Eddy had clung on around the corner, but the unexpected buck was too much. He flew off sideways into a dusty ditch.

Back on his feet quickly, Eddy shouted after Serenade.

Meridien was just coming round the corner, walking calmly. Lost in his thoughts and enjoying the view, Meridien had not noticed that his naughty friend had disappeared into the distance, trails of dust behind her.

Charlie saw Eddy on the ground, he was fine but flustered that Serenade had just disappeared and galloped up the hill. There was no choice, Meridien and Charlie had to go to the rescue. Meridien was no racehorse - Charlie knew that from her ride on the racetrack in Muscat, but he could cover the ground quickly with his long legs, much faster than Serenade with her short pony legs. Focused on the task at hand, Meridien and Charlie galloped off up the hill to find the naughty pony.

Serenade was hiding behind a hedge at the top of the hill. There was an open gate to a grassy paddock. She was snacking in there, surrounded by bleating sheep and looking very relaxed. She neighed to Meridien. That is how she gave away her hiding place!

Serenade never knew she had been naughty. It was just the way she was - very cheeky. Charlie took her by the reins, and she walked calmly alongside Meridien, back down the stony track towards the pub.

Eddy was huffing and puffing as he came up the hill. His smart white jodhpurs were now shades of dirty brown and dusty grey. He looked cross and was waving his wrist in the air, pointing to his watch.

'We are going to be late!' he shouted out to Charlie.

'Quick Eddy, hop back up into the saddle,' Charlie said, handing him Serenade's reins. 'We need to get back quickly to get you cleaned-up!'

Charlie added, looking at Eddy who was in no state to attend a wedding reception.

Charlie called ahead and a clean pair of jodhpurs were waiting for Eddy at the bottom of the hill. He changed quickly in the back of the horsebox. Charlie gave Meridien and Serenade a quick brush. Everyone was smart again. White ribbons flowing, they headed down a side road by the pub where the wedding reception was taking place.

They were late. All the guests had gone into the marquee already - but they could not leave again just because they had missed Judy arriving at the reception. They were there for Judy, a surprise on her special day. It was definitely going to be a surprise if they rode right into the marquee. Which they did! White Ribbons flowing, Charlie and Eddy rode Meridien and Serenade into the marquee and they *clip-clop-clip-clopped* across the wooden dance floor!

Judy's face lit up when she saw them. She came running over.

She was so happy to see her favourite pony and Meridien, there to share her special day marrying Tom, the lovely landlord from the pub close to Camels Bottom Farm. The lovely Tom who for months on end had baked Judy's favourite cake to give to her on her visits to the pub with Serenade, Charlie, Meridien, Eddy and Neddy. Eventually Tom had proposed to Judy by hiding an engagement ring in one of his cakes!

Tom ducked out of the marquee as soon as he saw the horses only to reappear a few minutes later with a big red bucket of water and a large bag of bright orange carrots. Meridien whinnied to Tom, happy to see him - and the carrots. Serenade started to paw the dance floor with her front left hoof. Eddy turned red with embarrassment.

'Stop it! I promise, if you are good, there will be carrots!' Eddy told the cheeky pony.

Meridien splashed his nose around in the water bucket, making all the guests laugh as he created quite a puddle on the dancefloor. He was not drinking the water but cooling himself off from the heat of the busy marquee.

Once Serenade had calmed down, Tom gave both the horses carrots. The wedding photographer ran around snapping this fabulous sight for Judy and Tom to keep as a memento of their happy day.

It was rather crowded in the marquee with Meridien and Serenade having joined the party. Charlie and Eddy said their farewells and wished Judy and Tom a happy wedding day.

Cheeky Serenade of course needed to leave her mark. There was a loud trumpeting sound. It was not an oompah band this time. Uh oh! Serenade could not hold it in. She dropped a steaming greenish brown package right in the middle of the wooden dance floor. Eddy turned red again. Everybody laughed. It was definitely time for them to leave!

Meridien and Serenade's appearance at the reception certainly made for a memorable wedding day for Judy and Tom!

Royal Treats

England

Meridien was not born into royalty, but, on his travels, he had become friends with the horses of the Old Palace Stables in Abu Dhabi, he had seen the Sultan and the Sultana in Oman, he had met the King of Orange and all his royal friends in the Netherlands and now he knew Neddy who had spent many years in the service of the Queen.

One day, Eddy, farmer Teddy's son, turned to Charlie as they were grooming the horses.

'Would you and Meridien like to visit Buckingham Palace?' he asked her.

Charlie jumped up and down with excitement.

'Wow, we would love to!' she replied.

Meridien and Charlie would never say no to a new adventure.

'Neddy has been invited by the Queen to a garden party,' explained Eddy. 'He's allowed to take a friend. As Meridien and Neddy get on so well - and Meridien can be trusted to behave - I thought it would be fun.'

'Meridien will be on his very best behaviour,' promised Charlie.

Eddy and Neddy had met the Queen many times. Meridien and Charlie had never met her. It was very exciting. Would they go there for tea? What would Charlie wear? What would she say? Would she have to curtsy?

On the morning of the big day, both horses were groomed and plaited. Charlie could almost see her reflection in their coats they were so shiny. Boots were buffed. Saddles were polished. Up the ramp the horses leapt. They were off to see the Queen.

From the side window of the horsebox Meridien got to see the sights: Big Ben, Houses of Parliament, Trafalgar Square with all the pigeons, Piccadilly Circus with the bright lights, beautiful bridges crossing the River Thames and lots and lots of people. So many people dashing about, chatting and laughing. There were people everywhere.

The horsebox turned into The Mall, the road leading up to Buckingham Palace. There were even more people. They all lined the side of the road, waving flags - Union Jacks, the flag of the United Kingdom. All waiting for their chance to  see the Queen. People came from all over the world just to catch a glimpse of Her Majesty. Meridien and Charlie were actually going to meet her.

They unloaded in the grounds of Buckingham Palace where there was a buzz of activity in the air. Neddy, the pretty palomino pony, and Meridien were very excited. As was Charlie.

'I know a top-secret route out of the Buckingham Palace gardens to Hyde Park,' Eddy told Charlie. 'Let's sneak through there and give the horses a chance to stretch their legs after the journey.'

Neddy and Meridien jogged excitedly through the gardens of Buckingham Palace and found the secret passage, which led to a busy road. What a lot of noise! Meridien was used to the quiet English country lanes. This was very different - it was chaos. There were cars, lorries and big red buses everywhere. Neddy had been there many times before and guided Meridien safely through the busy London traffic.

Quickly they were across the road and in Hyde Park, on a sandy track called Rotten Row, a special riding track for the Queen's horses. The park was packed. Children were playing, dogs were barking. There were joggers, cyclists and lots of tourists. People stopped to take pictures of the pretty palomino and the tall chestnut with the golden shimmer, Neddy and Meridien.

'Smile for the camera,' joked Eddy. 'We'll be on social media all around the world by the end of the day - we'll be famous!'

Charlie and Eddy giggled as they trotted off and let the horses burn off some steam before going to meet the Queen.

*

It was time for the garden party.

The festivities had started. All the people were wearing hats. There were other horses there too, horses Neddy had met before when he used to live in Windsor where the Queen has her famous castle.

Suddenly there was a very loud noise - it was like the oompah band in Austria, but the sound came only from trumpets. The trumpets that announced the arrival of the Queen.

All the people stood to attention, the horses too. Well, all except two big bay racehorses who were jogging on the spot and prancing restlessly, wound-up by the sound of the trumpets. Meridien whinnied to them, it was Whisper and Warrior, the horses with whom he had been on two long plane journeys!

Whisper and Warrior stopped their jogging and prancing when they heard Meridien calling to them. They whinnied back. They had come to join the

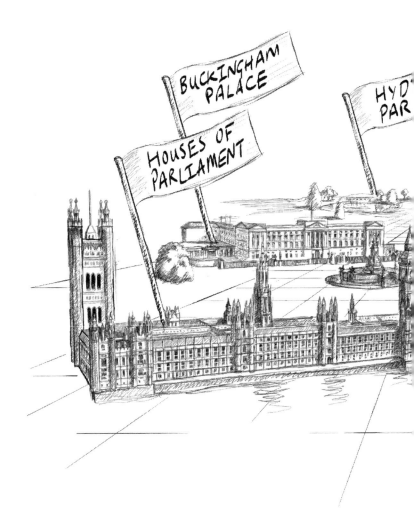

Queen's stable of racehorses. It really is a small world!

The Queen came straight over to the horses. She would meet the people later. The King of

Orange, wearing his bright orange tie, had come over from the Netherlands especially for the garden party. He accompanied the Queen. Each time she came up to a new horse she reached into a bag. The bag was full of perfectly peeled carrots.

When she came to Meridien, ready to give him a perfectly peeled carrot, the King of Orange turned to the Queen.

'I know this horse, Ma'am!' he told the Queen. 'He's the French horse who came to the King's Day party for my birthday. He likes dates from Abu Dhabi!'

Charlie and Eddy laughed. How amazing that the King of Orange remembered Meridien and his love of dates.

Meridien still got his perfectly peeled carrot from the Queen (he had never had his carrots peeled for him before - it was a royal treat!). Neddy got two perfectly peeled carrots as he was one of the Queen's favourite horses.

Once they had finished munching their perfectly peeled carrots, all the horses paraded around the Buckingham Palace garden for the people to admire as they sipped at their glasses of champagne. Neddy and Meridien joined Whisper and Warrior for the procession.

Then it was time to head back home, to leave the royal garden party. Time for Meridien to whinny farewell to his flying travel buddies, Whisper and Warrior - until the next time.

When they got back to the horsebox, there was a large parcel on the ramp. It was wrapped up in red, white and blue - in a Union Jack. Eddy went to investigate.

He turned to Charlie laughing.

'You will not believe this! It's a big box of dates! A gift for Meridien from the Queen!'

Meridien's nostrils were fluttering. He had already smelled the dates and was whinnying and nodding his head.

Epilogue

Meridien, the leggy foal with a big white blaze and three white socks, born in the green pastures of the Loire Valley in France has certainly had quite a journey so far.

All the castles and palaces he has seen.

The countries and continents he has visited.

The friends he has made along the way.

The treats he has collected in his travelling sweet shop: mints, dates, apricots, pomegranates, apples, pears, cherries, carrots, oranges and corn on the cob – but not bananas.

Flying, sailing.

Meridien the globetrotter.

Charlie had found the best travel partner and she knew they were so lucky to have seen so much of the world together.

She also knew that that there was still so much more to see!

Once a globetrotter always a globetrotter...

Travel Dictionary

Yallah! Let's go - now you can go to all the countries Meridien visited on his globe trot and greet people in their own language:

Ahlan: Arabic for Welcome.

As-salamu alaykum: A polite Arabic greeting - Peace be upon you.

Bonjour: French for Hello.

Grüß Gott: (you say: Gruess Gott) a typical Austrian greeting.

Guten Tag: German for Hello or Good Day.

Hoi: Dutch for Hi.

And you can say: **Yallah!**: Arabic for Let's go!

Horse Sense

Here are just a few horsey terms that you will have come across on Meridien's journey:

Arabian: an Arabian horse is a type of horse that originated in the Middle East. They are famous for their stamina and endurance. Very highly spirited and sprightly in nature they have a distinctive elegant, dished face.

Bay: the colour of Whisper, Warrior and Ticket. The colour ranges from light to dark brown but the mane and tail are always black.

Blaze: a wide white stripe down the middle of a horse's face.

Bridle: the combination of buckled straps that you put on a horse's head so you can steer and control the speed when you are riding.

Canter: one of the four paces, or speeds, of a horse. Canter is the third fastest after walk and trot, but it is slower than a gallop. It has a three-beat rhythm and is a very comfortable pace to ride (unlike trot!).

Chestnut: the colour of Meridien and Serenade. The colour, depending on the light and the thickness of the coat, can be from bright orange to a deep orange-brown or orange-gold.

Coat: a horse's coat is not a jacket! It is the horses' natural fur. It grows thicker and longer in the colder months of the year to keep the horse warm. It thins out naturally when the seasons change, so the horse is cooler in the warmer months.

Dressage: ballet for horses!

Forelock: the horse equivalent of a fringe.

Hand: one hand is four inches or 10.16 centimetres - the unit of measurement used to describe the height of a horse. It started out as being the size of a man's hand, an easy way to measure when you don't have a tape measure!

Hoof: a horse's foot. You say 'one hoof' but 'four hooves'.

Palomino: the colour of Neddy. The colour ranges from cream, through yellow-gold and the mane and tail are white or cream.

Saddle: the 'seat' that you put on the back of a horse to sit on when riding.

Socks: a horse doesn't actually wear socks! Socks are the markings on the legs of a horse that are about the length of long sport socks.

Stable: a horse's bedroom.

Trot: one of the four paces, or speeds, of a horse, trot is the second fastest after walk. It has a two-beat rhythm and is very bouncy!

Whinny: the soft sound a horse makes.

Travel Notes - Questions

What can you remember from
your travels with Meridien?

1) What is Meridien's favourite treat?

_____

2) In which country did Meridien go to a wedding?

_____

3) What colour is Meridien's HUGE suitcase?

_____

4) What is the name of Eddy's horse?

_____

5) What were the names of Charlie's doctors in the
hospital in Heidelberg?

_____

6) How many countries do you visit with Meridien in this book? Can you name them?

_____

_____

7) How do you say 'Hello' in French?

_____

8) What is the capital city of the United Arab Emirates?

_____

9) How do you say 'Let's go' in Arabic?

_____

10) What was the name of Meridien's friend in Heidelberg?

_____

11) What is the capital city of Austria?

_____

12) Which treat does Meridien not like?

_____

13) How do you say 'Hello' or 'Good Day' in German?

_____

14) What are the names of farmer Teddy's Labradors?

_____

15) Who still writes letters to Meridien?

_____

16) How many horses travelled together in the flying stable? Can you remember their names?

_____

17) What was the name of the plane that Meridien flew on from the United Arab Emirates to the United Kingdom?

_____

18) What are the three ways to get off an island?

_____

19) What was the name of the newspaper Meridien had his picture in?

_____

20) Can you name all the treats Meridien collected in his travelling sweet shop?

_____

All the answers to the above questions are found in the chapters of this book! But just in case, they are also on page 144.

BONUS QUESTION: What would you put in your travelling sweet shop?

_____

Travel Notes - Answers

1. Dates
2. England
3. Green
4. Neddy
5. Doctor Heart and Doctor Beat
6. Eight. France, Qatar, United Arab Emirates, Sultanate of Oman, England, The Netherlands, Austria and Germany
7. Bonjour
8. Abu Dhabi
9. Yallah!
10. Ticket
11. Vienna
12. Bananas
13. Guten Tag
14. Ready and Steady
15. Sophie
16. Three. Meridien, Whisper and Warrior
17. The Ark
18. To fly, to swim or to sail
19. The Oasis Times
20. Mints, dates, apricots, pomegranates, apples, pears, cherries, corn on the cob, carrots and oranges

About the Author

Claire is a lawyer who has always been passionate about everything she does. As a child she had a great love of horses and of travel. The theme of her tenth birthday party was a trip around the world. Her parents recreated the inside of a plane in their house and flew Claire and her friends to all the continents of the world, stopping to take in the sights of many different countries. It was an incredible experience that her friends still remember today, and it certainly made a mark on Claire, spurring on her enthusiasm to see the world.

She started riding as a young child and horses have been part of her life ever since. From the age of eight she would spend hours at the stables - mucking out, helping with lessons - just to be with horses and to get the chance to ride.

Through her career as a lawyer, she has been lucky enough to combine horses and travel.

Claire has always wanted to share some of her globetrotting experiences in the hope of inspiring others, especially children, to want to explore the world, to see the sights, to experience different cultures and to go off on their own globe trot - with or without a horse!

And that is how **Globetrotter - Meridien Travels the World** made its way into your hands to read.

About the Illustrator

Antony is an illustrator (obviously!), an author and artist. He and his wife live in a tiny village in North Yorkshire where he loves to illustrate, paint landscapes and portraits and write stories. Though he is surrounded by majestic horses grazing in the fields nearby, he has hardly ever ridden one, but he would love to, partly because he secretly fantasises about being a cowboy! So he was delighted when Claire got in touch to see if he would like to illustrate this book.

To find out more about Antony, please visit his website: www.antonywootten.co.uk.

Acknowledgements

The African proverb says it takes a village. Well, this book has taken people from many villages, cities and towns across the world to put together and I am exceptionally grateful to them all.

Meridien is the star of the show. He really is such a wonderful horse and a great travel partner.

Without my amazing parents, Alexandra and Dennis, I would never have had the opportunity to meet Meridien and travel to all these fabulous places. They have also been an incredible support on my journey putting this book together.

A big shout out goes to my incredibly supportive editing team of Isa in Germany, Alida in Australia and Sandy and Stu in England. A huge thank you to them all for their great ideas and their patience with me.

As a lawyer, of course I had my legal team, so a big thank you to James, Joanna and other legal acquaintances for putting up with all my questions.

A big thank you to Shah for his support on some of the cultural references in the Middle East and to May for the fabulous Arabic translation for the Oasis Times.

There are also a number of children I would like to thank for agreeing to listen to my story as it developed: Charlie, Carrie, Maddie, Sophia, Leon, Henry, Niesha, Jess, Amelia, Lila, Emily, Joseph, Ellie, Tess and Lucy.

There are many friends that I have met on this globetrotting and writing journey that have been a source of inspiration and others that have been patient with me as the book has come together. I thank you all.

Merci

Shukran

Dank je wel

Danke

Thank you

Keep in Touch!

Meridien always appreciates fan mail, by email or airmail. Of course, you can write to Charlie too as she will be the one reading your messages to Meridien.

www.meridientravelstheworld.co.uk

www.facebook.com/meridientravelstheworld

www.instagram.com/globetrotter__mttw

Printed in Great Britain
by Amazon

61743958R00095